Winter Pony

Winter Pony

by JEAN SLAUGHTER DOTY
Illustrated by TED LEWIN

SCHOLASTIC BOOK SERVICES
NEW YORK • TORONTO • LONDON • AUCKLAND • SYDNEY • TOKYO

ISBN: 0-590-10237-0

Copyright © 1975 by Jean Slaughter Doty. Copyright © 1975 by Macmillan Publishing Co., Inc. This edition is published by Scholastic Book Services, a division of Scholastic Magazines, Inc., by arrangement with Macmillan Publishing Co., Inc.

12 11 10 9 8 7 6 5   9/7 0 1/8

Printed in the U.S.A.

0 1

To Black Jack—
who loved the snow and
the sound of the bells.

Chapter One

"Hey, Mokey!" Ginny Anderson ran down the hill as she called cheerfully to her pony, a small bucket of hot mash swinging from one hand.

Through the twilight Mokey whinnied in answer. Ginny could hear the sound of quick hoofbeats, and Mokey appeared in a blurred pattern of brown and white as she trotted up to the paddock gate.

"Hi, Moke." Ginny stopped to give her pony a quick pat and then let herself into the small tack room in the stable, beside the paddock. She switched on the lights, unlatched the narrow door into the stall, and found Mokey waiting inside, peering into her feed tub as though waiting for her supper to appear like magic.

Ginny poured the sweet, hot mash into the tub, and Mokey plunged her muzzle deep into the swirling steam with a sigh of contentment.

Leaving the pony to enjoy her supper undisturbed, Ginny went to stand for a moment by the open stall door that led to the adjoining paddock.

The frosty twilight sky was deepening into purple and the evening star blazed brightly over a far ridge of trees. "Star light, star bright," said Ginny under her breath, and then stopped. There was no need to go on. For years she had wished on every star, ever since she could remember, for a pony of her own. Now she had Mokey, with her brown and white spots, her one blue eye and one brown, her black forelock and white mane and black tail—not exactly the beautiful pony of her dreams, but a real, live pony nevertheless.

Mokey was fat now and shaggy in her thickening winter coat. The new little stable had just been finished, painted a deep red with white trim. It smelled marvelously of fresh sawdust and drying paint, sweet hay, and pony.

Ginny squinted thoughtfully up at the evening star. It seemed hard to remember how thin and shabby Mokey had been just last spring, when she and her mother had found the pony at the Sweetbriar Pony Farm and rented her just for the summer; how the whole family had become so fond of the pony that they had been unable to let her go when the end of the summer came—

It was getting colder. Ginny shivered and went outside to close both halves of the heavy Dutch doors of the stall to shut Mokey in for the night.

Mokey finished her mash, slobbered a last happy mouthful over the front of Ginny's jacket, and turned to start on her hay. Ginny finished cleaning the stall, added fresh bedding, and filled the water bucket to the brim. The weather report had predicted a hard frost for the night. Ginny brought out Mokey's new winter blanket and buckled it on.

"You greedy thing," Ginny said to her pony. "This blanket fit just right when we got it for you, and now I have to loosen the back surcingle. You're getting fatter every day." Ginny smoothed the pony's mane and gave her an affectionate pat. "Saturday tomorrow," Ginny said. "We can be out all day. And you sure need the exercise to work off some of that tummy!"

Ginny bolted the narrow door behind her as she left the stall and stood for a happy moment in the tack room, checking to see that everything was in its place. Bales of hay, and shavings for bedding, were neatly stacked at the back of the room. The ceiling lights glowed on the dark leather of the halter and bridle on their racks on the wall, the white cotton lead ropes, and the buckets and metal storage cans for grain under the shelf where the brushes and grooming things were kept. The pitchfork, rake, and broom were hung on the wall where they belonged. Humming softly under her breath, Ginny switched off the lights and latched the door behind her.

Saturday dawned clear and bright, but it was the middle of the morning before Ginny could escape from the house. "Not an inch," her mother had said firmly after Ginny had given Mokey her morning feed and had finished her own break-fast. "You are not stirring one inch from this house, young lady, until you tidy your room!

Honestly, Ginny, how you can keep your stable so neat, and your room such a disaster area . . . !"

Ginny couldn't explain, either, as she flung things into her drawers, made her bed and, feeling slightly guilty, kicked an old notebook under the bed. Cleaning up her room was a chore and taking care of Mokey was fun. It was as simple as that. She snatched her hunt cap from the shelf, tugged on her jacket, and ran down to the stable at last.

She was supposed to meet Pam Jennings at her place in fifteen minutes. Ginny brushed Mokey quickly, gave her a pat and a promise to do a more thorough grooming job the next time, bridled the pony, and started on her way.

Mokey knew where they were going; though she never minded being ridden alone, she always enjoyed going out with Pam's chestnut pony, Firefly. She broke into an eager trot and then into a strong canter. There were patches of silver frost on the shaded path through the woods and the air was crisp with the cold. Mokey gave a happy buck and a kick, and flourished her long black tail.

Ginny pulled Mokey back to a quiet walk as

they turned into the Jennings's stable yard. She had expected to see Pam on her pony, waiting, but the yard was empty and no hoofprints ruffled the smooth raked gravel in front of the wide white doors.

Ginny slipped off Mokey's back just as Pam started to roll back one of the doors. "Hi!" she said to Ginny breathlessly. "I thought I heard you coming, and then Firefly started to whinny, so I knew it was you. Come on in."

Ginny led Mokey into the sunlit aisle between the two rows of box stalls. Firefly whinnied again from his stall and Mokey whinnied in answer.

"Gosh, what a racket," said Pam, putting her hands over her ears. With their greetings over, the ponies quieted. "I'm sorry, Ginny, I tried to call you in time," Pam said when she could be heard again, "but you'd already left, I can't ride Firefly today."

"What's the matter? Is he sick?" said Ginny anxiously.

Pam glared at the closed door of the tack room. "Michael's such a fusser," she said crossly. "Firefly's got a tiny cut on his fetlock, you can hardly see it, but Michael's got that dumb pony wrapped up in enough bandages to keep a hospital going for a year. . . ."

She stopped and flushed guiltily as Michael, who was not in the tack room at all but just down the aisle with one of the other horses, came limping out of the stall.

Michael was lean and strong and had ridden steeplechasers in England before a bad fall had given him a permanent limp and put an end to his racing career. He was still able to ride and care for horses, and when Mr. Jennings had bought two hunters from him in England several years ago, he had persuaded Michael to come with the horses to school them and care for the others in his stable.

"Now, Miss Pam," he said crisply, "that cut's not much at the moment, but it will leave a scar if it's not cared for." Michael nodded to Ginny and went into the next stall.

"Glass," Pam said bitterly. "That pony is made of glass. Every time he gets the littlest lump or bump or bruise he practically ends up in slings."

"Never mind," Ginny said consolingly, "we'll have lots more days to ride together this winter.

It's not as though Mokey's going to be leaving, so it's not the same as it was last summer."

"That's true." Pam's face brightened. "I guess I got in the habit of feeling each ride was going to be our last. Now that Mokey is really yours, it makes a difference, doesn't it?" She gave the pony a hug.

"I don't really want you to fall on your head again," she said to Ginny, "but it sure was fun having Mokey here and taking care of her when you couldn't ride those few weeks. You're not planning to break a leg or something this winter, are you? Just so I can have her here again?"

Ginny grinned. "Not right away," she said. "It's much too nice having the new stable finished and Mokey home again. My father got the last of the shingles on the roof two days ago, and it's all done just in time for the cold weather."

"Too bad." Pam ruffled Mokey's forelock cheerfully. "Ginny, if you've got a minute, come see what Michael's been working on this morning."

Ginny slipped a spare halter over Mokey's bridle, cross-tied her in the aisle, and followed Pam into the warm tack room at the end of the stable.

Chapter Two

A row of darkly gleaming bridles hung high on one wall over a lower row of saddles protected by fitted linen dust covers. There were bright hunting prints on the other walls, and glass-doored cases of horse show ribbons and silver trophies. Ginny and Pam went into an adjoining room where Michael was whistling under his breath as he worked near a sinkful of steaming water. In the center of the cleaning room, on a heavy hook hanging on a chain from the ceiling, was the most confusing jumble of black leather that Ginny had ever seen.

"Isn't it beautiful?" said Pam enthusiastically.

Ginny ran her finger doubtfully over the glowing black leather. "I'm sure it's wonderful," she said at last, "but what is it?"

"It's a harness!" said Pam. "Look, here's the bridle." She lifted it off the hook and Ginny recognized the blinkers of a driving bridle, though she'd never seen one quite like this before, even in pictures. The blinkers were shining patent leather and on each of them was a delicate silver monogram. The brow band was also patent leather, and fastened over it was a chain pattern of square silver links.

"Mother used to show driving ponies," explained Pam, turning the bridle in her hands so that the silver twinkled and glowed. "That was ages ago, of course, before she married my father and they started showing hunters instead. She kept this harness because it was one of her favorites and Michael keeps it in the storeroom and gets it out to oil and clean it now and then. It's in terrific condition, isn't it? I wonder if anyone will ever use it again."

"If you take good care of nice leather, it lasts for years," said Michael. "But not if you leave it outside on a fence rail and let horses chew on it." He frowned at Pam, took part of the harness off the hook, and went over to the sink.

"Oh, dear," whispered Pam. "He's still mad about my leaving Firefly's halter out in the paddock last week. I thought he'd forgotten about it by now." Pam sighed. "What do you want to do this morning, Ginny? Do you want to go on riding without me? It's a shame that dumb pony of mine had to wreck himself on a Saturday after we've waited through a whole week of school for a good long ride."

Ginny had been looking forward to spending the day with Mokey, but she didn't like to leave Pam with nothing to do. She hesitated.

Suddenly Pam whirled, the driving bridle still in her hand. "Michael!" she said excitedly. "Wouldn't this fit Mokey?"

Michael considered the harness thoughtfully. "Probably would," he said. "The last pony your mother drove was her bay Hackney and he was just about Mokey's size." He frowned through the steam with the soapy sponge still in his hand. "Now, Miss Pam, don't you go getting any of your crazy ideas. You can't just throw a harness on a pony's back and drive it away. There's a lot more to it than that, and it takes some time to break a pony to harness."

He turned back to the sink with a firm shake of his head. "And, what's more, the pony cart can't be used. A friend of your father's borrowed it and the shaft was cracked when he brought it back."

"Darn." Pam slumped down on a stool and put her chin in her hands.

Ginny felt a sharp stab of disappointment. She'd often wondered what it would be like to drive a pony; it looked like fun. And to be able to drive a pony of her own—

Pam jumped to her feet. "Let's harness-break her anyway!" she said. "Michael, you'll show us how, won't you? You keep saying what wonderful manners Mokey's got, and how sensible she is. She'd be terrific in harness, wouldn't she? And then maybe we could get the shaft fixed—"

"Miss Pam, by the time that cart is able to be used, there'd be snow on the ground and then you couldn't take it out anyway," said Michael.

Pam grinned triumphantly. "Then I'll get the bells," she said. "Where are they, Michael?"

Even Michael had to smile at her excitement. "Wrapped in a gray flannel bag in the top drawer of the storage chest," he said. As Pam whirled out of the room he let the water out of the sink and dried his hands. "I think I'm in for it this time," he said. "But Mokey is your pony, Miss Ginny. Do you want to teach her to drive?"

Ginny was confused; she didn't understand what Pam and her bells had to do with Mokey and the harness, but she nodded her head determinedly. "It would be great," she said, "if Mrs. Jennings says it's O.K. for us to use her harness."

"Shouldn't wonder," said Michael. "It's good for tack to be used. But we'll ask her, of course, before we start." He shook his head in amusement. "Anything to keep you two girls from moaning around the stable, getting in my way."

But Ginny knew he didn't mean it. Michael seemed as pleased with the idea as she was. Pam came racing back into the tack room accompanied by a shimmering, tinkling sound from something she was holding hidden behind her back.

"Just look," she said to Ginny. "We've got a sleigh and these are the bells." And she handed them to Ginny.

Ginny looked at the bells in speechless delight. There were three of them mounted on an arched metal stand, and with every slight movement of her hand they chimed with a silvery, whispering sound.

"Have you ever seen anything so pretty in your entire life?" said Pam. "They fasten to the harness in the winter when you're driving a sleigh. I don't know how, but Michael does. Oh, Ginny, wouldn't it be fun to go sleighing this winter? It's something I've always wanted to do, but we never had a pony who was broken to harness to pull the sleigh before—at least, not since I can remember!"

"Neither will you this winter, if you don't get on with it." Michael took the bells from Ginny and put them on a shelf. "We'll not need these for a while yet. The two of you can polish these up some rainy afternoon while you wait for it to snow. In the meantime, you both have a lot to do."

Chapter Three

It seemed to take forever before Michael finally was satisfied with the way the harness fit Mokey. Ginny held Mokey in the stable aisle while Michael tested and fitted each strap and buckle. He moved slowly, letting Mokey get used to the feeling of each piece of harness before he added another.

Pam disappeared and then came back with the news that her mother was pleased that the harness was to be used, as long as it was done under Michael's supervision, and that she looked forward to being given a ride in the sleigh.

"If he ever gets done with all this before the snow thaws next spring," whispered Pam crossly under her breath as Michael went to get a leather punch to shorten a strap.

Ginny patted Mokey and smiled at Pam's impatience. Mokey moved her head uncertainly; the driving bridle felt strange to her.

Finally Michael was done. "Right," he said with satisfaction. "Lead her down the aisle and back again." He stepped back and nodded to Ginny. Ginny clucked to Mokey. The pony took a step or two forward, then suddenly skittered to one side, bumped the wall and plunged into Ginny, almost knocking her down.

"Ouch!" said Ginny, hanging desperately onto Mokey's bridle. She managed to make the pony stand still. Rubbing her shoulder where the heavy driving bit had bruised it, she frowned at Mokey. "What was that all about?"

Mokey's eyes were rolling in a peculiar way and she was standing with her back humped up. "She's not used to the feeling of a harness," said Michael. "And it startled her when she moved. Pat her and talk to her. Now try again."

Mokey snorted her protest and gave a half-hearted kick as she started to walk again, but soon she became familiar with the feeling of the harness on her back and paid no more attention to it.

"Outside with her now," said Michael, rolling

back the wide white stable door. Ginny led Mokey out into the stable yard and led her at a walk and trot until she was scarlet in the face and out of breath and Mokey was bored.

"Very good," Michael said at last. Ginny took Mokey back inside the stable and Michael took the harness off and put it back on again several times. By this time Mokey paid no attention to any of the straps dangling and tapping against her hindquarters and flanks. Certain that none of these things was going to hurt her, she half-closed her eyes, relaxed one hip, and stood dreamily in the sunny aisle while Michael showed Ginny how to put the harness on by herself.

"That should do it," Michael said at last. "We'll do the same tomorrow."

"You're kidding!" said Pam. "What about putting the reins on the bridle? What about—"

"That's enough for one day," Michael said firmly. "Slow and easy does it, Miss Pam. Hurry has no place with horses."

"Let's go look at the sleigh," suggested Pam after the harness had been returned to the tack room and Michael had shooed the girls out of his way. "It's in the storage barn beyond the paddocks. It's been there for years; I don't know when it was last used."

The two girls both got on Mokey and trotted bumpily down the lane which ran between the white-fenced paddocks. Ginny held Mokey while Pam tugged at the doors of the barn. They finally opened with a shriek of hinges. Inside, in the dim gray light that filled the old hay barn, a small red sleigh with delicately curled runners stood in a corner.

"It needs a new paint job, but Michael said he'd been down here and checked it just a little while ago and it's in good enough condition to be used," said Pam. Mokey was reluctant at first to walk into the barn with its wooden floor, which made a funny noise under her hoofs, but after a little bit of coaxing, Ginny managed to lead her over to the sleigh.

"Gosh, it's a pretty thing," said Ginny with awe in her voice, running her hand over the curve of the shaft. "It looks just like a Christmas card."

Mokey blew softly down the back of Ginny's

neck as the two girls and the pony stood admiring the little sleigh in silence. "Well," said Pam finally, "it's going to be absolutely terrific, but I'm sure glad you started breaking Mokey today. Otherwise, with the way Michael does things, it would have been the middle of next summer before Michael said she was ready!"

The next day, and every chance she had after school and on weekends, Ginny worked with the slightly puzzled but willing Mokey under Michael's watchful eye. The long driving reins were run through the rings on the harness and buckled

to the bit; Ginny learned how to hold them, and how to manage the light driving whip at the same time.

At first it was hard for Mokey to understand why Ginny was walking so far behind her, instead of being up on her back where she belonged. The pony walked ahead of Ginny as though she felt lost. But as the days went by, both Ginny and Mokey began to feel more sure of themselves.

Ginny groaned one evening after dinner as she got to her feet. "You wouldn't believe how stiff I am!" she said. "I've walked *miles* today!"

"I thought you were teaching that Moke of

yours to drive," said her father. "Why all the walking? No wheels?"

"No wheels," said Ginny. "Just me on my legs and Mokey on hers. Even if we had any wheels, which we don't, we still wouldn't be using them because Michael says Mokey and I don't know enough."

At the next practice session Michael fastened the traces of the harness to a log which had a sturdy ring bolted onto each end. "Watch your pony," he said to Ginny as he stepped back out of the way. "She may not like the sound of the log dragging behind her."

Ginny nodded and clucked to Mokey, who took a step and then stopped, puzzled by the feeling of pressure as the traces tightened. Ginny clucked gently again and touched the pony lightly with the whip. Michael came to lead the pony forward and the log moved with a grating sound over the ground.

Mokey raised her head and clamped her tail between her legs. But Michael and Ginny both spoke to her reassuringly, Ginny's hands were gentle and steady on the reins, and the brief moment of worry was soon over.

"I don't know who has the most patience," said Pam wonderingly to Ginny. "You or Michael or Mokey." She jumped down from the stable yard wall where she'd been watching. "I'd be bored to death by now."

Ginny just smiled without speaking. It took a lot of concentration, but the pony was walking steadily now, paying no attention at all to the bumping drag of the log behind her. With a tiny flourish of the tip of her whip, she drove Mokey out through the gates and down the lane between the paddocks.

Relaxed and obedient, Mokey walked and jogged ahead of Ginny, stopping and starting smoothly whenever she was asked and making circles and turns evenly and without hesitation.

Everything had gone well.

By the end of that afternoon, as Ginny rode Mokey home through the gathering dusk, she knew that both she and Mokey were ready.

Chapter Four

Michael thought so, too. The sleigh was brought up from the barn. Michael replaced a loop of cracked leather and rubbed leather conditioner into another, and oiled the bolts which fastened the shafts to the sleigh. Ginny and Pam dusted and polished the old, chipped paint as well as they could, helped to push the sleigh into a small shed near the stable, and waited anxiously for snow.

Ginny had to be content with riding Mokey alone. The cut on Firefly's leg had healed perfectly but he celebrated by bucking Pam off the first day he was ridden. Racing back to the stable, he slipped and fell as he turned through the gates, slid on the rough gravel and ended up back in bandages again.

The weather grew colder. Ice formed in lacy patterns at the edges of the streams, and the blacksmith welded rough metal on Mokey's shoes the next time she was shod. "Just a touch of Borium on the toes and heels to keep her from slipping on the ice or packed snow," the blacksmith explained. "Got to keep at least one of these ponies on its feet!" and he went to pull the shoes off Firefly, who didn't need to wear them while he was confined to his stall.

But still there was no snow. Ginny took Mokey out in harness at least once a week to keep in practice, but even she and Mokey were beginning to be bored and it wasn't as much fun any more. Thanksgiving came and then the short vacation was over. Ginny and Pam listened eagerly to the weather reports and squinted hopefully at the sky every morning before they went to school. The ice skating was the best there had been in years as the ponds froze smoothly in deep, black ice with the surface unmarked by snow.

The ground froze until it was as hard as concrete and Ginny's rides became slow and dull, as the footing was too hard and rough to do much more than walk or jog slowly. Mokey grew fatter and shaggier every day, but still there was no snow.

"Let's move to Canada! Or the Alps or the North Pole!" Ginny said furiously the next Saturday morning as the sun rose in a bitterly cold but cloudless sky. "There's got to be snow for the sleigh *somewhere* in the world!"

She stomped bitterly down the hill to feed Mokey, who was whinnying loudly for her breakfast. Ginny had forgotten to put her gloves on and her hands hurt as she pulled back the metal bolts and swung the doors open that led from the stall to the paddock. Mokey came charging out with her tail in the air, whistling through her nostrils and greeting the cold morning with a buck and a kick of delight. Ginny shook her head gloomily. With her cold hands shoved into her pockets she watched her pony prance cheerfully across the paddock. It was all very well for Mokey to be so bright and gay, but the stall needed a thorough cleaning—Ginny had skimped a little through the week, as there'd been exams almost every day— and the wheels were probably frozen on the manure cart, and a newly delivered bag of grain had split open and spilled, and the hoofpick had vanished and simply must be found . . . . Ginny sighed and went to get Mokey's grain. Firefly was still lame and Pam had gone skiing. It was going to be a long, dull weekend.

The alarm clock buzzed. Ginny flung one hand out from under the warmth of the blankets and slapped at the clock. It fell over and became silent.

Ginny groaned and opened her eyes. Monday morning. Yuk. She pulled the blankets up over her head and tried to remember whether or not she'd corrected her math paper over the weekend.

Even through the muffling blankets she could hear the clink of dishes and the sound of running water in the kitchen. She'd better get up and feed Mokey if she wanted to get it done before breakfast.

She stumbled sleepily out of bed and wandered, shivering, across the room. With an enormous yawn, Ginny started to get dressed.

Her arms and back were stiff. Ginny cleared her throat experimentally. There were a lot of colds and things going around school at this time of year. Maybe she was coming down with something. Maybe she was getting sick and wouldn't have to go to school today, after all.

She coughed hopefully and then sighed. She knew very well she was stiff because she'd ridden for long hours the day before and she also knew she had not done her math. Gloomily, she tugged a sweater over her head.

Her mother tapped lightly on the door and opened it. "You might as well go back to bed," she said. "No school today!"

"No school?" Ginny's head shot through the tight neck of her sweater and she stared at her mother.

"Just look out the window." Ginny's mother smiled. Suddenly wide awake, Ginny flew over to the window and pushed back the curtains.

It must have snowed all night. It was still snowing hard. Drifts billowed across the lawn, buried the small bushes in the garden, and rippled smoothly across the driveway.

"Beautiful," Ginny said out loud. *"Beautiful!"* She snatched up a sock and stood, hopping on one foot, looking out at the snow. From the kitchen she could hear the murmured sound of the local radio station report: All schools in the area closed for the day due to the unexpected heavy storm.

"Hear you have a snow day today!" her father greeted her as Ginny came into the warm kitchen. "Why don't you go back to bed?"

"Bed!" Ginny said in horror. "But it's snowing!"

Her father smiled; he'd only been teasing. The radio was now giving the weather report: Up to six inches of snow expected to fall before stopping at noon; clearing during the afternoon, with sunshine expected, and slowly rising temperatures.

"Perfect," said Ginny with a shiver of excitement. She drank a glass of orange juice, pulled on her snow boots and jacket, and plunged outdoors into the snow.

All the world smelled cold and clean. The snow swirled everywhere, silently heaping the tree branches and filling the air with dancing patterns. With the flakes melting on her face, Ginny ran down to the stable to give Mokey her breakfast.

Pam was on the phone, wild with excitement, when Ginny got back to the house. Ginny promised she'd be over just as soon as she could. "But I've got to wait an hour after Mokey's had her grain, and she's just been fed," Ginny said. "Do you think Michael will remember to put the bells on the harness?"

"I'll remind him," said Pam, "just in case. See you soon!"

Ginny was as impatient as Pam, and the hour passed slowly. She had a quick breakfast, brushed and rebraided her hair, shoveled snow away from the garage door with her father, and watched him drive away with the tire chains jingling on the rear wheels of the car.

At last it was time to get Mokey. The eager pony danced through the snowy woods, following the slight tracing of the familiar path through the trees. The woods were full of mystery and a gentle, hushed silence; there was no sound of hoofbeats; nothing but the whispering of the snow sifting through the trees and Mokey's soft breathing. The snowflakes fell like powdered sugar on Mokey's black forelock and over the hood of Ginny's jacket. As the snow swirled around them in the close silence of the woods, Ginny thought dreamily that this must be what it would be like to be a tiny figure inside a crystal ball—the kind that filled with snow when it was shaken and turned.

She was almost sorry when the ride was over, but her heart jumped with excitement as Pam slid the stable door back to welcome Ginny and her snowy pony inside.

No one said very much. Pam was sparkling with suppressed excitement; Ginny concentrated silently on fitting the harness in place. And Michael had not forgotten the bells. They rang lightly as Ginny finished and Mokey started to paw the ground with anticipation.

Ginny hesitated. "Are you sure it's all right for the harness to get all wet in the snow?" she finally asked Michael, who had been watching without comment. "Maybe we should wait until it stops."

"Silly," said Pam with a giggle before Michael could answer. "In the olden days, do you think people stayed home if it snowed? Horses and carriages went out in all kinds of weather!"

"Pony's going to be all right," Michael said

briefly. Ginny felt a little better. Michael understood; now that the moment had finally come, Ginny was nervous. Mokey suddenly looked big and unfamiliar in the black and silver harness. The snowy fields and lanes outside no longer looked soft and inviting; they looked threatening and full of hidden dangers. Maybe they hadn't practiced enough. Maybe the bells would frighten the pony.

Ginny knew if she waited one more moment, she'd never be able to go through the critical moment of actually fastening Mokey's traces to the sleigh. Barely giving herself time to pull on her gloves, she nodded quickly to Pam and led Mokey outside.

Pam had pulled the sleigh from the shed and it was waiting in the stable yard. With Pam holding the pony, Ginny helped Michael ease the curved red shafts through the loops of the harness. Ginny was shivering so hard that her teeth chattered. She tried to follow Michael's quick hands as he fastened the traces and buckled the harness to the sleigh, but she was much too nervous, and there were too many things to remember.

32

"I'll teach you to do this another time," said Michael. "But this first time out, we don't want to keep the pony standing any longer than we must."

He straightened up, checked one last buckle, then stepped back. He and Ginny looked at the waiting pony and the pretty red sleigh in a moment of silence.

"Oh, come *on!*" said Pam as Mokey tossed her head and made the silver bells ring. "Aren't you ready *yet?*"

Chapter Five

Ginny's throat was so dry she could hardly swallow. "In you go," Michael said to her. "Gently, now." He went to Mokey's head and held her while Ginny stepped quietly into the sleigh and gathered the reins and the whip in her hands.

It felt very strange and awkward to be sitting so high and so far away from Mokey. Ginny gulped again. Michael spoke softly to Mokey and turned to look at Ginny questioningly. Ginny nodded stiffly, Pam stepped back, and Michael clucked to the pony.

Mokey took one step, but as the traces tightened against the weight of the standing sleigh, she stopped uncertainly. "Come on, Mokey!" Ginny said hoarsely; Michael patted the pony and clucked again, and the pony lowered her head and moved forward.

Once it was started, the sleigh slipped silently and effortlessly through the snow. The bells on the harness chimed softly. Once they were safely through the stable yard gates, Michael stepped away from Mokey's head and the reins came alive in Ginny's hands. She felt Mokey's mouth with the reins through the bit and the pony responded and turned down the lane leading between the paddocks.

Mokey was walking more freely now and with more certainty. "Miss Pam," Michael said quietly, "you walk by the pony's shoulder for a bit. If there's any trouble, you be ready to take hold of her head. Otherwise, let her alone." In one quick and silent movement he was in the sleigh beside Ginny. Wordlessly Ginny handed the reins to Michael. The snow fell and stung her face, the harness bells rang softly, but Ginny didn't notice. She was too busy watching Michael's hands on the reins and listening to what he said. They drove at a quiet walk down the lane, made a wide sweep around the old storage barn, and started back toward the stable. They passed the gates, went around the wide sweep of driveway in front of the Jennings's house, and, once past the stable yard again, Michael let Mokey move on into a jogging trot.

Pam, by now, was completely out of breath. At Michael's nod, she flung herself down on a snowbank and waved as the sleigh went on. Mokey was moving evenly and with more sureness. Michael nodded with crisp satisfaction.

"Good," he said. Ginny glowed.

Michael drew Mokey back to a walk. "Here you go," he said to Ginny, and handed her the reins.

At the feeling of different hands on the reins, Mokey threw her head up and stopped. Michael was out of the sleigh and at the pony's head before Ginny even saw him start to move.

"Gently, little lady," he said to the pony reassuringly. He led Mokey for a few minutes and then swung silently back into the sleigh.

Ginny's hands grew stiff with cold and tension; her head whirled as she tried to remember everything Michael had taught her; the tracks of the sleigh runners, which had run so straight when Michael drove, snaked and wobbled uncertainly behind them as she drove her pony down the lane. Mokey, feeling the nervousness in Ginny's hands, kept stopping, and once she tried to back up, but Michael was always quick to move to her head to get the pony moving forward again.

Gradually the telltale marks of the sleigh runners started to straighten out. Michael was in the sleigh now more than he was out of it and, once or twice, he even nodded his approval as Ginny managed a wide turn with the pony moving evenly between the shafts.

The moment finally came when Michael stepped out of the sleigh and gestured to Pam. Her dark eyes shining with excitement, Pam slipped silently onto the red leather seat beside Ginny.

Mokey broke into an easy jog and the silver bells rang. Dimly Ginny heard the gentle murmur of the bells and the hushed hiss of the runners through the snow. The reins began to feel comfortable in her hands and Mokey trotted strongly and cheerfully along the drifted lane, her breath making twin puffs of steam in the cold air.

As they started to sweep past the stable yard again, Michael shook his head and raised his hand. Reluctantly Ginny drew Mokey back to a walk and then to a stop. Michael went to the pony's head and gave her a lump of sugar. "Very good, Miss Ginny. Very nice indeed. But your pony's had enough for one day."

Guiltily Ginny became aware of the clouds of steam rising from Mokey's sweating sides and noticed how heavily the pony was breathing. She jumped quickly out of the sleigh and helped to

lead Mokey into the stable yard; Pam ran to get a cooler which she threw over Mokey's back. Together the girls covered the hot pony with the wide blanket to keep her from getting chilled while Michael unharnessed her from the sleigh.

Ginny had thought she was tired when she'd gotten out of the sleigh. But by the time Mokey had been unharnessed, taken into the stable to be rubbed and walked and then rubbed again, she felt as though she could never take another step again. Pam helped by taking over Mokey's cooling out, but then there was the heavy harness to be carried into the tack room where every salty sweat mark had to be saddle-soaped clean under Michael's watchful eye. Even the bit and all the buckles had to be dried and polished back to their original shine before Michael finally allowed her to hang the harness in its place in the tack room.

Ginny collapsed onto a hay bale in the stable

aisle and sighed wearily as Michael ran his hand over Mokey's chest and shook his head in disapproval. "Pony's still warm," he said.

"But Michael!" Pam said with a wail. "Her coat's so long it's *never* going to dry out!"

"This is always a problem with an unclipped pony," said Michael. "And that's why she tired so quickly. I'd be happy to clip her for you, Miss Ginny, but you won't be able to turn her out in the paddock for very long during the day without the protection of her winter coat. And while you're in school, you can't very well be there to let her in or out of her stall as the weather changes."

They all surveyed the shaggy pony in silence.

"But you might consider a New Zealand rug," said Michael. "It's a special blanket made of canvas and lined with wool. It's windproof and waterproof, and especially made to be worn as a turn-out blanket. An ordinary stable blanket isn't strong enough for this."

Ginny made a face. She'd already learned this; she had let Mokey out into the paddock wearing her blanket one cold morning. By noon one of the webbing surcingles was torn and one of the two leather chest straps was broken. It had taken a week to have it mended, and she knew better than to do it again; the blanket came off before the pony went out.

"I suppose they're expensive," said Ginny.

Michael nodded sympathetically. "But they do last for many, many years."

Ginny frowned at Mokey. "I hope you're worth all this," she said. "I've been saving my allowance for a long time for a portable radio. But I think I'd much rather have a New Zealand rug for Moke." She got stiffly to her feet. "We've been trying to get her cooled out and dry for almost two hours, and I just can't bear the thought of ever having to go through this again, no matter how much fun it is to drive her in the sleigh!"

"I'll take her for a bit," said Michael. "She's almost done."

Gratefully Ginny followed Pam up to the house where the two girls curled up in front of an open fire in the study and sipped steaming mugs of cocoa.

"You know what?" said Ginny, squinting her

eyes and dreamily watching the steam curl up out of her mug. "It all looks so simple in the Christmas cards, doesn't it? Jingle bells, put the pony to the sleigh and away we go. Nothing about harness-breaking the beasts or learning how to drive them or cooling them out and cleaning all that harness afterwards. Do you realize the hours —the absolute *hours* we spent working for that one morning of sleighing?"

She shook her head wonderingly. "Not that it wasn't worth it. It was wonderful, and I can't wait to go out again. But it does make you stop and think a little." There was an old English coaching scene in a heavy gold frame over the fireplace. Ginny looked at it briefly and shuddered. "Four horses, can you imagine? All that muddy harness—"

"—and four hot, dirty horses to cool out and groom and put away," said Pam with a smile. "Here, you'd better have another cookie. You've still got to have enough energy left to ride Mokey home."

Chapter Six

The New Zealand rug was ordered from the tack shop and, after it had been delivered, Michael clipped Mokey.

Without her shaggy winter coat the pony looked very strange and bare to Ginny. And Mokey's back was more slippery and harder to stay on, Ginny found, as she rode the pony home again in the late afternoon. Mokey wasn't behaving very well, which didn't help. Every time Ginny asked her to trot, the pony humped her back and skittered sideways, and the first attempt at a canter sent Mokey off into a series of bucks and kicks that very nearly put Ginny off.

Cross and out of breath, Ginny quickly pulled Mokey back to a walk. The pony acted as though something was bothering her, like a twisted girth; but since Ginny was riding bareback, as she always did, this didn't make much sense. It wasn't until Ginny got home and turned Mokey out into her paddock that she understood what had been causing the problem. As Mokey trotted unevenly across the paddock to her stall, Ginny could see that snow was kicking up from the pony's hoofs and tickling her on her newly clipped stomach. Ginny laughed out loud at the pony's insulted expression, knowing that Mokey would soon get used to it.

Wednesday was half-day at school, but Pam had a missed piano lesson to make up and couldn't ride. Michael gave Ginny the message when she rode Mokey over to the Jennings's stable and then offered to spend the afternoon teaching Ginny how to harness her pony to the sleigh. It was warm and sunny in the sheltered stable yard; Mokey stood patiently, half asleep in the sun, while Ginny fiddled with the straps of the harness, but it didn't take long. Within a short time they all made sense to her and she could manage to harness and unharness the pony without Michael's finding a single mistake.

Ginny finished up by driving the sleigh alone, feeling more and more sure of herself and of her pony. But the snow was getting soggy in the sun and the sleigh would no longer slide easily.

"But we're in great shape now," Ginny reported to Michael as she finished cleaning the harness and went into the tack room to put it away. "Mokey's clipped, I know how to harness her to the sleigh by myself—all we need now is more fresh snow."

Ginny got her wish. Christmas vacation started with a two-day storm. The flurry and the excitement of the holidays slipped by quickly, and it snowed again on New Year's Eve. When Ginny rode Mokey over to Pam's the next morning, the sky was still dark with the look of more snow to come.

Ginny found Pam raging up and down the aisle of the stable. They had planned to go riding in the fresh snow that morning, but Firefly had developed a cough during the night. Michael had stated firmly that the pony could not be ridden and had gone off to visit a friend.

"Do you want to go out in the sleigh again,

since you can't ride Firefly today?" Ginny suggested.

Pam scowled and kicked at a snowbank in the yard. "I suppose so," she said finally. "But it's pretty dull now, isn't it? I mean, just going back and forth in the lane and in the driveway. We've done that lots of times. I don't see why we can't take the sleigh out on the roads."

"Usually they're plowed and salted," Ginny reminded her. "And the snow melts too fast, especially when the sun comes out, and then there's not enough snow left for the sleigh."

"But there is today," said Pam eagerly, "and it's going to snow again. Come on, let's do it. Think what fun it would be."

Ginny hesitated. "I don't think Michael would let us," she said at last.

"Oh, fiddle," said Pam impatiently. "He's an awful wet blanket. You know that. Don't do this, Miss Pam, don't do that, don't ride your poor pony today, he's got a little cough—worry, worry, worry. That's all he does." She shook her short, curly hair impatiently. "Come on, Ginny, I'm so bored! There's nothing else to do! We don't have to go very far if you don't want to."

46

Ginny straightened Mokey's black forelock and smoothed it over the browband. "O.K.," she said at last. After all, it was Pam's sleigh, not her own. It seemed the least she could do, if Pam wanted it so badly. And Ginny had to admit to herself that it *was* getting a little boring just driving around the Jennings's place—

Ginny pressed Mokey's bridle reins into Pam's hand. "I'll go and get the harness," she said.

The runners of the red sleigh slipped easily over the packed snow on the road. Mokey reached lightly for the bit, flourished her long black tail, and lengthened her stride. The silver bells on the harness made a brighter sound than they ever had before.

The snow-laden branches of the trees arched over them as they spun along the narrow, winding road. There was no sound anywhere but the cadenced chiming of the bells and the hushed whisper of the runners on the snow. It began to snow again, softly. Time stood still. They had gone several miles before Ginny realized suddenly how far they were from home.

"We'd better find a place to turn around pretty soon," she said, brushing the snowflakes from her face and pulling Mokey down to a walk. "The road's too narrow here to turn a sleigh. That was great, wasn't it?" she grinned at Pam. "This was a wonderful idea."

The road forked at the bottom of the hill. Ginny swept the sleigh around in a wide circle, glancing back with proud satisfaction at the evenness of the marks the runners left in the snow. Mokey broke into an amiable jog which set the

bells tumbling softly as though they were singing to themselves.

Pam sighed happily. "I heard somebody say once that whatever you do on New Year's Day you'll do all year long," she said. "I sure hope the rest of the year is as much fun as this."

Ginny didn't answer. Her hands tightened on the reins. Something was wrong; Mokey had raised her head and stiffened her back. Her ears were pricked forward in alarm.

"Hang on," Ginny said to Pam in a tight voice. "I don't know what it is, but something's scaring Mokey—"

The two girls knew in a moment. They heard what Mokey had heard several moments before— the low, muffled roar of an approaching snow plow.

Pam's face went white. She clutched frantically at Ginny's arm. "What are we going to do? We're going to be killed!"

"Let go of me!" Ginny said sharply. "I can't drive with you hanging onto my arm!" She shortened the reins. Mokey had broken stride and had dropped back to a faltering walk.

The snow plow was on the road somewhere ahead of them, hidden by a bend in the road. Mokey had broken out in a nervous sweat. Her head was moving from side to side and she kept trying to stop. Ginny knew that the frightened pony was getting herself ready, gathering herself to whirl around and run away from the terrifying roar that was coming closer all the time. But with all the storms they'd been having, the banks were piled high on both sides of the road with plowed snow, and there simply was not enough room to turn the sleigh around.

Chapter Seven

The glowing headlights and flashing red warning lights of the plow swung into view at the far end of the road. Mokey reared in fright. Above the hysterical clashing sound of the harness bells Ginny could hear Mokey's hind shoes slipping as they cut through the snowy surface, down to the icy road underneath. For one terrifying moment Ginny thought Mokey was losing her balance and was going to fall backward onto the sleigh.

"Hang on!" Ginny cried to Pam as Mokey caught her balance and started to rear again. The bells jangled harshly. The thin driving whip whistled through the air, just once. Startled and surprised, Mokey plunged forward.

The sleigh jolted and swayed. Ginny was shouting, and Mokey was galloping—straight toward the terrifying plow.

They could see the white plumes of snow curling away from the wide blade of the plow; the flashing lights grew brighter through the falling flakes as they got closer. Mokey was weaving crazily back and forth across the road, but Ginny was doing the only thing she could think of to do. Not far ahead, just beyond a snow-heaped clump of rhododendron bushes, she remembered having seen a driveway. If she could just keep Mokey going, they could reach the driveway in time to get out of the way of the plow.

Mokey skidded to a sudden stop and tried to rear again. Pam shrieked and Ginny shouted and the pony plunged forward again. There was a low bank of snow across the entrance to the drive, but there was no time to slow down. Ginny steadied her pony as well as she could and then swung her into the drive.

There was silence. There was cold and darkness everywhere. Ginny lay perfectly still. She couldn't open her eyes, everything was black, and she was afraid to try to move.

Dimly she heard the gentle chiming of bells. At least she knew that Mokey wasn't lying dead in the snow with a broken neck; dead ponies didn't ring sleigh bells. Having decided this, Ginny felt better and struggled to sit up.

No wonder everything was cold and dark; she'd landed face down in a snow drift. Ginny blinked, brushed the snow from her face and looked around quickly; whatever awful damage had been done, she had to know.

Pam was sitting in the snow next to Ginny. Her head was in her hands and her shoulders were shaking under her red jacket.

Ginny jumped to her feet in alarm. "What's the matter? Where are you hurt?" she asked in a shaking voice. Muffled gasps and choking sounds came from Pam and she looked up at Ginny with tears in her eyes. "I never saw anything so funny in my life!" she said, and Ginny realized furiously that Pam was laughing.

Ginny whirled to see what was so funny. She didn't know that she herself was covered from head to foot with snow and that she looked like a walking snowman. Mokey was standing peacefully in the drifted driveway, clouds of steam rising from her sweaty sides. The red sleigh was half tipped over behind her at a peculiar angle, the reins were curling in dark tangles all around her legs, and she was pawing delicately at the snow to see if there was any grass to eat underneath.

"I'm sorry, Ginny. I didn't mean to scare you." Pam gurgled helplessly. "But you really looked so funny with your feet sticking up out of the snow, and wouldn't you know Mokey would try to find something to eat at a time like this?"

Still half angry, Ginny walked stiffly over to Mokey, who turned her head and reached over to Ginny's pocket, begging for a lump of sugar.

Ginny fumbled in her pocket, found the damp lump of sugar Mokey had known was there, and gave it to her absently while she looked the pony over and then checked the harness and the sleigh.

Ginny took off one glove and ran her hand over Mokey's legs, feeling for cuts or bruises, but she couldn't find any. Pam, looking contrite but still giggling occasionally, came to hold the pony while Ginny finished examining the sleigh. It took only a light push to set it back on its runners.

"Lead Mokey forward a few steps to see if she's all right," Ginny told Pam. Mokey moved through the snow without any trouble and Ginny shrugged her shoulders. "Nothing seems to be wrong," she said, almost crossly, and found she was yelling to be heard; the snow plow was going by the entrance to the drive where they stood. The flashing lights made orange and red flickering patterns on the snow and then it was gone, leaving a high mound of white where the entrance to the drive had been.

"Oh, great!" Ginny said furiously. "*Now* what are we going to do? We're going to be stuck in here until spring!"

"The driver could hardly have known we were in here," Pam said reasonably, gesturing toward the roar of the receding plow. "I'm sure he never even saw us."

Ginny rubbed Mokey gently between her ears. "I'm sorry," she said apologetically both to Mokey and to Pam. "I didn't mean to sound so mad. I was so scared, and I just couldn't believe everything was all right—" Pam smiled understandingly. Ginny gave Mokey another lump of melting sugar and squinted through the falling snow, surveying their problem.

There was no question about it. They really did have a problem. Mokey and the sleigh were facing away from the road. The driveway where they stood had been plowed at some time earlier in the winter, but not recently. The snow was knee deep all the way to the house, which was set so far from the road that they could barely see it.

"It looks as though there's just flat lawn here beside the driveway," said Pam. "We can't do any damage to it with Mokey's hoofs at this time of year, the ground's too well frozen. The way that house sits down in that little hollow the snow may have drifted pretty deep. Maybe we should try to turn around right here."

Ginny looked at the level snow doubtfully. Anything could be hidden under its surface. A low wire fence, or a forgotten toy wagon, or even a narrow, ice-bound stream with sharp, rocky banks—

She shivered. "We can't stay here forever, and Mokey's getting cold. We'll just have to try it and be very careful, I guess."

Pam walked ahead to feel for hidden obstacles under the snow and Ginny followed, leading Mokey. They made a wide circle and triumphantly stopped where they'd started but facing, this time, toward the road.

"Now all we have to do is get from here to there," said Ginny, feeling more cheerful until she had another long look at the towering wall of fresh snow between the pony and the road.

Pam scrambled up over the drift and then came back. "It's soft," she reported. "At least it's not icy, but it's pretty deep. Do you think Mokey and the sleigh can get through?"

It was Ginny's turn to laugh. "I don't think we have much choice," she said. "We're going to have to try." She climbed into the sleigh and took a deep breath. "You lead Mokey to get her started," she said to Pam, "but be ready to jump out of the way if the sleigh tips over."

"O.K." Pam patted Mokey encouragingly, clucked to the pony, and started toward the drift.

Mokey plunged forward determinedly. Pam cheered her on. The pony hesitated when the snow suddenly started to get deeper, but quickly

surged forward again. Mokey floundered through the deep drift but the sleigh rose up behind her as though lifted on the crest of a wave. The delicate sleigh lurched and swayed as it reached the top and for one sickening moment Ginny was sure it was going to tip over. But Pam steadied Mokey with her voice and her hands; the pony braced herself and the sleigh dipped forward and slid gently and evenly down onto the freshly plowed road.

"Wow," was all Ginny could say.

Pam grinned. "I should imagine," she said as she got into the sleigh beside Ginny, "that must be what it's like to launch a lifeboat in a storm."

Mokey turned her head to look back at the two girls. "I think," said Ginny, "she's suggesting we go home."

"Terrific idea," said Pam. Ginny shortened the reins and clucked to her pony; Mokey set out at an even, smooth trot and the bells began their soft chime.

It was cold enough so that the plow had left a thin layer of snow on the road, though the runners bit through to the road surface occasionally with a grating sound that made the two girls and the pony give a startled jump each time.

It was with an enormous sigh of relief that Ginny steadied Mokey back to a quiet walk and turned her into the Jennings's drive.

"Not a word of this to Michael," Pam said warningly.

Ginny giggled. "Do you think I'm out of my mind?" she said. "Anyway, he doesn't have to know we've even been off your place! We could have just been puttering around here as we always have before. Unless we tell him, how could he ever know?"

Mokey was hot and tired. Guiltily Ginny let her walk slowly, hoping the pony would look cool enough and rested by the time they reached the stable.

"Yuk," said Ginny under her breath as they started down the lane that led to the stable.

"What's the matter?" asked Pam.

"Just look who's there," answered Ginny, nodding toward the stable yard gates.

"Oh-oh," said Pam. "And I can tell, even from here, he's *furious*."

Michael stood waiting, standing with his hands on his hips, looking very steely and grim. He nodded coldly, just once, as Ginny drew Mokey to a smooth stop at the gates. Ginny hoped he might comment on how nicely she'd stopped—in fact, she wished nervously that he'd say just about anything at all, just to break the chilling silence.

But Michael just nodded shortly once more as he stood looking at the weary pony and the uneasy girls in the sleigh, then turned and went into the stable without a word.

Pam sighed. "I have never," she said slowly, "in all the years Michael's been here, gotten away with one single thing without his knowing all about it." In silence they unharnessed the pony, threw a cooler over her back and took her inside the stable before putting the sleigh away and carrying the sweat-covered harness to the tack room. They hung it on the cleaning hook and started working on it with hot soapy sponges.

There was no sign of Michael. Ginny scrubbed vigorously at the bit, glancing over her shoulder occasionally. "Whew." Pam stopped working for a moment and pushed the hair back out of her eyes. "There's a mile of this thing, isn't there!"

Ginny nodded silently. She looped the straps and tucked them into place as they were cleaned until, at last, the whole harness was done and hung back in its place.

Pam folded the cooler as Ginny quickly bridled Mokey and swung up onto her back. Pam looked around quickly as she opened the door to let Mokey and Ginny walk outside, then whispered, "I don't care how mad Michael is. It was fun, anyway!"

Ginny waved good-by, happily grateful to escape without having encountered Michael again. Mokey was very tired. As soon as they reached the path through the woods, Ginny got off, pulled the reins over the pony's head, and led her toward home. It was getting colder and starting to snow heavily again. Ginny made a face at the lowering clouds. Even she and Mokey, she decided, had had enough snow for a while.

Chapter Eight

"You look worried," Ginny's mother said.

"I am," said Ginny. She was stirring bran and oats and scalding water together into a hot mash she was making for Mokey in the kitchen. Thoughtfully she added a little salt and put a folded towel over the top of the bucket to let the mash steam. "Gosh, that stuff has a wonderful smell," she said. "No wonder ponies love it."

She started to cut up a carrot to add to the mash. "I'm worried about Mokey," she said to her mother. "I can't understand what's the matter with her. She's fit, and I feed her well, but her ribs are starting to show a little bit even though her blanket hardly goes around her middle."

"What does Michael say?" asked Mrs. Anderson.

"He just told me she was getting too fat and that I was probably giving her too much hay. But he told me that when he first clipped her, before Christmas, so I did give her less hay, and now she looks kind of strange. He's gone back to England to visit his family for a few weeks, so he hasn't seen her for a while.

"Thank goodness," she added under her breath. Nothing had ever been mentioned about the sleigh ride on the road on New Year's Day. Maybe, by the time he got back, he would have forgotten all about it.

"Do you think it might be a good idea to ask the vet to have a look at her?" suggested her mother. "Ginny, for goodness sakes, don't give Mokey *all* the carrots! We need some for the salad tonight!"

"I'm sorry." Ginny grinned at her mother and quickly put the cut-up carrots into the mash. "I'll go call Dr. Nichols and ask him to come see Mokey."

Dr. Nichols came the next afternoon and left an hour later with a smile and a cheerful wave.

Ginny clomped into the living room, forgetting to take off her snow-covered boots, and stood numbly in front of the fire.

"You'll never guess what," she said with a croak to her mother and father. Her father put down his newspaper and her mother looked up from her book.

"Mokey's in foal," said Ginny.

"In foal?" said her mother.

"You mean she's pregnant?" said her father. Ginny nodded speechlessly.

Mr. Anderson folded his newspaper and began to laugh. Ginny scowled at her father. "It isn't funny!" she said, and then she began to smile. "I guess it is, at that," she said. "Imagine her being in foal all this time, without our knowing anything about it!"

"When is she due to have it?" asked Mrs. Anderson.

"Dr. Nichols says it's hard to tell with horses and ponies, especially with a first foal, but he thinks probably toward the end of March or the beginning of April. She probably was bred just before she came here, and it takes eleven months until the foal is born." Ginny shook her head wonderingly. "I can't really believe it yet. I keep thinking I'm dreaming."

She glanced down at the snow from her boots that was melting on the living room rug. "Help!" she said breathlessly. "I'd better get out of here. And I've got to call Pam!"

Pam was wild with excitement and envy. "I've always wanted to raise a foal!" she said.

"You can share Mokey's," said Ginny. There was a short silence as both girls tried to picture Mokey with a foal. Ginny found it impossible.

"I can't wait to tell Michael," Pam said with a giggle. "Mokey sure fooled him! I'll bet this will be the biggest surprise of his life!"

But Michael took the news quite calmly when he came back from his vacation. It was a chilly, cloudy afternoon when Ginny rode over to the Jennings's on Mokey. It had started to rain and then the rain turned to sleet. Ginny put Mokey into the extra stall and went into the tack room with Pam to welcome Michael home and to tell him the news.

66

Michael nodded as Ginny told him. "But she did fool you, didn't she, Michael?" said Pam.

Michael smiled at her. "Miss Pam, there's a lot of horsemen been taken by surprise by a lot of mares for a lot of years. When I was just a lad I worked for one of the best trainers in England. He knew more about horses than anyone I've ever met, before or since. He had a young filly run a great race one afternoon—she either won it or was second, can't remember which—and when they went to see to her the next morning there was a foal at her side, standing up and nursing just as bright as you please. Took some time for him to live that one down, you can be sure."

"You mean the filly was racing fit and still the foal didn't show?" said Ginny. "Oh, come on, Michael, that's hard to believe!"

"Any harder to believe than that a pony you've cared for all these months has kept her foal a secret from you?" asked Michael.

"I see what you mean," Ginny said reluctantly.

"I can name you two ponies in the show ring today, and one show hunter and a jumper, which were just as big a surprise to their owners when they were born," said Michael. "Sometimes a dealer will breed a flighty mare to settle her down and then sell her quickly without telling anyone what's been done. Sometimes the breedings are accidental; a fence gets broken down, a stall door is left unlatched at the wrong time, the mare or the stud gets loose—the boy who's responsible for the horses whisks them back to their stalls, and who's the wiser? He's not going to admit he was careless and risk losing his job."

"Were there any stallions at that awful place where you got Mokey?" asked Pam.

"Oh, sure," said Ginny. "There was at least one. A chestnut, with a lovely head and a narrow white blaze. He nearly bit Mr. Dobbs, which would have served him right. There might have been some others, too, but Mr. Dobbs didn't say."

"Well, there you are," said Michael comfortably. "Not really such a surprise, is it? Man like that, doesn't care one way or another about his ponies, probably turned them all out together without a second thought. You ask your vet, Miss Ginny. He'll tell you this kind of thing happens all the time."

Dr. Nichols agreed with Michael when he stopped by a few days later with a vitamin-mineral supplement for Ginny to give Mokey in her feed.

"But it still seems kind of unreal," said Ginny.

"Don't put Mokey's blanket on tonight before you feed her," Dr. Nichols said. "Very often you can see the foal kick when the mother drinks water or eats her grain, but a blanket would hide this. Put your hand on her flank, if you want to be absolutely certain; you can feel the foal move, even if you can't see it."

Ginny fed Mokey early that evening and as Mokey eagerly plunged her muzzle into the fresh grain, Ginny, feeling a little foolish, put the palm of her hand on Mokey's flank, just in front of the pony's hind leg, as the doctor had told her to do.

When she felt a sudden flutter under her hand she jumped back as though she'd been stung. Feeling even more foolish, she put her hand back on the pony's flank again. This time she held it there, and the flutter ended in two strong bumps against her hand before it stopped.

Mokey turned her head to look at Ginny, who looked back at the pony in a haze of delight. "It's

real," said Ginny. "I felt it, I really did. It's true."

Mokey sneezed contentedly and went back to her grain. Ginny went to get the blanket and then stopped to give her pony a hug and to press her face into the white shaggy mane. The sun set behind the ridge and the stall filled with twilight shadows. Mokey finished her grain and turned to her hay.

Ginny gave Mokey a final hug. "I don't even care whether it's a colt or a filly, or how many silly spots it has," Ginny said as she finished buckling the blanket into place. "But Mokey, it would be nice if its eyes matched!"

Chapter Nine

As the first weeks of early spring went by, the frozen ground began to thaw. The icy ruts of the lanes and paths turned into deep and heavy mud. The red sleigh was put back in the old hay barn and the silver sleigh bells were taken from the harness, polished one last time, and stored away in their gray flannel bag.

The days lengthened and grew warmer. Ginny heard the liquid call of mourning doves when she fed Mokey in the mornings before she left for school, and snowdrops bloomed in the sunny corner beside the kitchen steps.

Ginny rode over to Pam's one day and the blacksmith took Mokey's shoes off, trimmed her feet, and tossed the shoes into the back of his truck.

"Good little mare," he said approvingly to Mokey. "Had us all fooled, didn't you?" Mokey closed her eyes dreamily while the blacksmith and Michael compared stories about unexpected foals.

"Are you sure it's okay for her not to wear shoes?" Ginny asked the blacksmith anxiously as Michael went to bring Firefly from his stall.

"Vet says she's getting near her time, doesn't he?" said the blacksmith. "Then no more shoes for a while. An unshod hoof does a lot less damage should a mare step accidentally on her foal."

Ginny shuddered. She watched while the restless Firefly was shod and turned out into a white-fenced paddock to buck and play in the light spring wind. "I'm glad I'm not on him today," Pam said. "He gets higher than a kite when the wind blows like this." She and Ginny walked back to the stable with Mokey trailing along behind at the end of the reins. "How much longer can you ride Mokey?"

"Dr. Nichols says she ought to be exercised," said Ginny. She looked back at Mokey doubtfully. "But she's getting absolutely enormous. Maybe she's going to have twins."

"Can horses have twins?" asked Pam.

"I think so," said Ginny. "Let's ask Michael."

Michael said that horses and ponies could indeed have twins, but that it didn't happen very often and that it was unusual for twins to live. "One's enough, anyway," said Ginny, making a face. "I just wish it would hurry up and come. All this waiting makes me nervous."

"I don't really understand what all the fuss is about, anyway," said Pam. "Ponies have foals all the time. Except this one is pretty special, I guess, because it's Mokey's."

"There you are," said Michael. "That's it exactly. Everything looks different when you come down to the individual mare."

Ginny looked miserable and then her eyes filled with tears. "I wish all this had never happened," she said in a shaking voice. "It seemed so wonderful at first, but now I'm scared. Suppose something goes wrong?"

"Wild ponies have foals all by themselves, without anybody around to help," said Pam.

"That's true," said Michael. "But some of those mares die, and some of those foals as well. It may not matter in the long run to the survival of a wild herd, but it can matter a lot when it's one Thoroughbred broodmare foaling what may be the future winner of the Derby, or when it's your own pony having her foal."

Ginny nodded speechlessly.

"It would be wrong for me to say that you shouldn't worry," said Michael. "A little constructive worry never did any harm. Chances are, nine times out of ten, Mokey won't have a bit of trouble. But the thing to do is keep an eye on her and telephone the vet when she first goes into labor. The foal will probably be born before he even gets there, but if the mare's in any trouble at all, he'll be there in plenty of time to help."

Ginny sniffed. She felt a little better. "I was beginning to feel sort of stupid," she said. "Everybody keeps telling me I'm making too big a thing of this."

"I never told you that," said Michael. "And neither did Dr. Nichols, I should imagine."

"That's true," Ginny admitted. "He's told me all kinds of things to do and not to do, but he's never said I could just forget about it."

She wiggled up onto Mokey's back and pushed a stray lock of the pony's white mane over onto the right side. She waved good-by and started the ride home. The bridle paths were so muddy that Ginny rode home on the road instead. Mokey's bare hoofs made a soft, pattering sound as she walked quietly along the side of the road. A motorcycle went by with a shattering roar, trailing a thick blue plume of exhaust. Mokey shook her head and shied a little.

"It's a good thing you're not like Firefly," Ginny said to her pony with a giggle. "You're so round right now I can barely stay on you at a walk!"

A few days later, when Ginny opened the stall door that led out into the paddock, Mokey came out with her head and tail in the air and trotted lightly across the muddy ground. Ginny stared at her for a bewildered moment and then peered hastily into the stall. Even though Dr. Nichols had assured her that the pony was not yet quite ready to foal, maybe he'd made a mistake and maybe Mokey had fooled all of them again. Ginny felt a guilty flash of relief. Much as she wanted to see the foal born, it would be wonderful to have all the waiting and worrying over and done with.

She looked carefully in every corner, but there was no spotted little foal curled up anywhere in the stall.

She went outside to look at Mokey again. She couldn't understand it. Mokey had been moving so heavily for the past few weeks, and now she was trotting around almost like her old self. But she was still enormously round, and as Ginny fed the pony, she could see the foal moving and kicking vigorously.

Puzzled, she called Dr. Nichols. "That's fine," he said. "We're making progress. The foal has changed position. It's moving down and Mokey feels less pressure. It's getting ready to be born."

"But I've got to go to school today!" Ginny said with a wail. "Will it be born today?"

"Today, tomorrow, or three weeks from now," Dr. Nichols said cheerfully. "It still can be quite a while. Tell your mother to let me know if she thinks she needs me at any time."

It was agony to get on the school bus that morning. Ginny's mother had promised that she would not leave the house and that she would check Mokey every hour through the day until Ginny got home from school. Though this helped a little, Ginny spent a miserable day. She telephoned at recess and at lunch, and her mother reported that Mokey was just napping quietly in the sun in front of her stall as she always did at noon.

By the time Ginny got home that afternoon, having run all the way from the bus, she was frantic and out of breath. Nothing had happened; Mokey was just as fat and cheerful as ever. "I'll go get some marketing done," said Mrs. Anderson to Ginny as she came into the house, "now you're here to keep an eye on things. We're all going to have to change our schedules for a while, I can see that! I won't be long—I don't want to miss the great event either!"

Chapter Ten

The last few days of school dragged by impossibly slowly, and then spring vacation started at last. "It's just as well," Ginny whispered to Pam that night. "I can't remember one single thing I've read in the last two weeks except the foaling chapters in the vet books I got from the library."

Pam just murmured a sleepy answer. She had come to spend the whole vacation with Ginny so she could be there to see the foal born, and she was almost asleep in the other bed in Ginny's room. Restlessly Ginny slipped out of bed and went to the window.

It was very late, and the night was crisp and cold. Ginny pulled on her bathrobe and tiptoed downstairs. She slipped her bare feet into her fleece-lined boots, put her ski jacket on over her bathrobe, and made her way down to the stable.

Since Mokey had been clipped but could not wear her blanket this close to her foaling time, Ginny's father, at Dr. Nichols's advice, had fastened several heat lamps high on the walls of the stall. The soft red glow from the lamps spilled out of the window; it had looked kind of spooky at first, almost as though the stall were on fire, but everyone soon got used to it and the lights kept Mokey warm.

Ginny looked through the window into the stall, trying not to disturb her pony. The heat lamps gave enough light for her to see that Mokey was lying down; she looked as though she were sound asleep, but the pony heard Ginny. She always did. She got to her feet, stretched, yawned, and came over to the window to press her muzzle against the wire mesh that protected her from the glass.

All was well. Ginny said a soft, "Good night, Moke," and went back up to the house.

"I don't see how anybody survives all this," Ginny said crossly a few days later. "Mokey's supposed to foal at any moment, Pam and I are taking turns getting up every two hours all night, every night, and neither of us feels as though we've slept for a month. It all seems hard to believe. The suspense is terrible."

Michael had come over to see how things were progressing, and he clucked sympathetically.

"I can share the night watch," said Mrs. Anderson. Ginny sighed. "Thanks anyway, but Pam and I can do it. We can manage. It can't be too much longer."

"That's what you said a week ago," commented Pam. She was sitting on an overturned bucket by the feed room door with her chin in her hands and her eyes shut. "Why don't we just skip one night and catch up on our sleep?"

Michael grinned. "If you do, I can promise Mokey will foal that very night."

"It seems so strange that anything as big as a pony can go into labor without any warning signs at all," said Mrs. Anderson.

"It does indeed," agreed Michael. "But even on the big breeding farms where they watch the mares day and night in the foaling barns, there's been many a foal born when the night watchman just slipped out for a few minutes for a cup of coffee."

"It doesn't always happen that fast though, does it?" asked Pam.

"Not always," said Michael. "Just often enough."

Pam yawned. "Mokey is smart enough to take naps," said Ginny's mother. "I think you two girls had better follow her example. I'll take the maternity watch this afternoon."

"I think Mokey's made the whole thing up," muttered Ginny. "I think she's just enjoying the whole thing as a joke." Mokey wandered back into her stall to eat more of her straw bedding.

Ginny and Pam slept all that afternoon and felt much better that evening. They cleaned the stall and fed Mokey. While the pony was eating, Ginny peered hopefully at the pony's swollen udder.

"She's got milk, I'm sure," Ginny reported to Pam. She patted Mokey encouragingly on the shoulder. "You've kept us waiting long enough," she said firmly. "Vacation's almost over. Have it tonight."

Mokey turned her head and slobbered bran mash on Ginny's shoulder, managing to get one of Ginny's braids full of wet bran as well.

Sighing, Ginny plodded up to the house to wash her hair.

But by Sunday evening Mokey still had not foaled. Almost in tears, Pam had to go home because school started the next morning.

"I could *scream*," Ginny told her mother between clenched teeth. She dragged her math book out from under her vet book and made a face. "How can I concentrate on this stuff all day at school? It isn't fair!"

Ginny's mother and father were sympathetic but firm. School came first; the chances were, anyway, that the pony would foal at night when Ginny was home; Dr. Nichols and Michael and the vet book all said so, though they couldn't be positive, of course—

Ginny knew all this and it didn't help at all. On Monday morning it was all she could do to drag herself out of bed, feed Mokey, and start her own breakfast. The cereal tasted soggy and stale. She pushed it aside and drank her milk. She shuddered. It tasted heavy and sour.

Ginny's mother hurried out the door, giving her daughter a quick kiss and a promise that she would be back in less than an hour so that she could watch Mokey for the rest of the day.

Ginny gathered her books together and glanced at the clock on the kitchen wall. Almost time to leave for the bus. She groped in the pocket of her jacket for her gloves and remembered she'd left them in the stable that morning on top of the oat bin.

With an exasperated sigh, Ginny tramped tiredly down to the barn.

Mokey was still eating her breakfast. She rattled her feed tub cheerfully as Ginny poked her head though the door to say good-by. For the hundredth time that morning, Ginny looked her pony over for any sign of approaching labor: the muscles hollowing on either side of the tail which sometimes showed to give warning, or the waxy substance which sometimes appeared to show that the first milk was ready—

Nothing. Ginny sighed and turned away.

As she started to close the door, she saw Mokey raise her head as though she were listening to a faraway sound. Then the pony turned, circled once in her straw bed, and quietly lay down.

Ginny stood motionless at the stall door, stunned by surprise. Mokey never left her feed until every last grain had been finished, and she never lay down during the day except for the nap she took at noon outside her stall door when the sun was high.

Mokey got up, pawed the straw uneasily, circled the stall and lay down again.

Her hands shaking with excitement, Ginny shut the door, hurried outside to shut the doors leading into the paddock, and then raced up to the house.

She flung her books on the floor and dove for the telephone in the hall. Dr. Nichols's receptionist answered the phone; the doctor was in surgery, she said, and could not come to the telephone; could she take a message?

"Tell him that I think Mokey's in labor!" Ginny said frantically.

There was a silence that seemed to last forever,

and then the receptionist's cool voice said, "Dr. Nichols will be there just as soon as he can." Even through her excitement, Ginny understood that the doctor could hardly leave another animal in the middle of an operation. Hurriedly she dialed the number of the Jennings's stable. Pam had already left for school and the boy who often came to help Michael with the horses answered the stable phone and reported that Michael was out exercising Mr. Jennings's hunter. He promised to give him the message about Mokey as soon as he came in.

Ginny hesitated, snatched a pad and pencil from beside the phone, scribbled the word "Mokey" on it, and propped it against the sugar bowl on the kitchen table so her mother would see it as soon as she got home. Then she ran back down to the stable.

Chapter Eleven

Mokey whinnied loudly at the sound of Ginny's footsteps. When Ginny opened the door to the stall, she found the pony was up on her feet looking bright and unconcerned.

Ginny glared at Mokey furiously. "What a dirty trick," she said in a shaking voice. "You've made me miss the school bus for nothing at all. Nobody's going to believe for one minute that I really thought you were in labor—"

Ginny stopped. She had been so surprised and disappointed to find Mokey standing up, and then so worried about what her parents and teachers were going to say, that she hadn't noticed at first the fresh light sweat on the pony's flanks.

"Oh, Moke," Ginny said softly, "you've got me

in such a spin over this whole thing that I can't think straight. It *is* time now, isn't it?"

Mokey made a soft whuffling sound, poked her nose against Ginny's jacket, and turned away. Ginny watched in silence as the pony moved restlessly around in her stall and pawed at the straw.

Ginny forced herself to move slowly. She took a long, shivery breath. The uncertainty had vanished and Ginny felt, instead, a peculiar calmness like the hushed stillness before a thunderstorm. She wished there were someone with her, but it couldn't be helped. She was alone with Mokey, the foal was coming, and there was nothing more she could do but wait.

She sat down on the fresh pile of hay in the corner of the stall. Mokey switched her tail, poked her side uneasily with her muzzle, and lay down. A ripple of muscles moved across her flanks. The first contractions had started.

The contractions grew stronger. Mokey lay with her legs curled under her and she rested for a few minutes with her head outstretched and a dreamy, faraway look in her eyes. Ginny moved a little to ease a cramp in one leg and Mokey's eyes flew open. She turned her head to look at Ginny and then struggled to her feet.

Ginny murmured soothing, meaningless words. A dog barked somewhere and Mokey spun around, tense with fright. Ginny got up and shut the stall window. She went on talking to her pony until Mokey began to lose her look of alarm. Gradually she relaxed, circled her stall slowly, and lay down again.

Ginny's mouth felt sandy and dry. She swallowed with a gulp and tried to recapture the calm she'd felt a few minutes before, but it was no use. All the stories she'd heard or read about mares in trouble foaling whirled sickeningly through her mind. She wanted to run out of the stall, she wanted to call Dr. Nichols again, or Michael, or *someone*—Ginny had never felt so alone in her life.

She stood at the side of the stall and jammed her sweaty hands into her pockets. Mokey let her breath out with a soft puff from the force of a contraction and Ginny's heart jumped with a sudden surge of excitement. The tip of one tiny hoof had appeared—then there was another—one more contraction, and there was the tip of a small muzzle looking blurred and out of focus behind the covering membrane.

"If you can see two front hoofs and the muzzle of the foal, you will know its position is good." Ginny remembered Dr. Nichols telling her this. More contractions; the foal's entire head and neck appeared and Mokey rested again.

Ginny couldn't believe it. Somehow she had thought that once the foal started to be born, all of it would come in a rush. But nothing was happening. Everything was still. There was such an unmoving silence in the stall that Ginny could hear nothing but the pounding of her own heart.

The contractions started again. Mokey was breathing hard and Ginny's knees were starting to shake. She knelt in the straw beside the pony trying to remember some of the things she'd been told. "Don't interfere; let nature take its course; don't bother the mare unless absolutely necessary." But what was the difference between interference and helping? Where did one change into the other? Ginny felt tears running down her cheeks; she didn't know what to do.

She heard the door opening quietly behind her and then Michael's low voice filled the stall with warm, reassuring sounds that drove away the terrible silence that had seemed so frightening. Through her tears, Ginny began to giggle. Michael's voice had the same tone she used herself when Mokey was afraid.

"Time to lend a hand," said Michael, coming calmly into the stall.

Ginny stood up, feeling dizzy with relief. "I don't know when I've been so glad to see anybody," she said in a hoarse whisper. She moved away from Mokey.

The pony turned her head and nickered softly to Michael before another strong contraction took her breath away. Ginny waited for Michael to move forward and, when he didn't, she looked up at him with a puzzled frown. "Aren't you going to do something?" she said.

Michael looked back at her gravely. "Wouldn't you rather do it yourself? You can't learn any younger," he said.

Ginny glanced at Mokey for one bewildered moment, hesitated, and then knelt again beside the half-born foal. "O.K.," she said briefly. "Tell me what to do."

She heard Michael's voice as though it were coming from a long way off, but it was clear and quiet. "The foal doesn't seem to be in trouble yet; neither does the mare. But what you're going to do now is just help things along a little, because somewhere along the way the foal stops getting oxygen through the umbilical cord—right this moment he's between one world and the next. Take hold of his forelegs and then pull when the next contraction comes."

Ginny's hands were shaking. She didn't know what to expect. The membrane around the foal looked strange and slimy. Ginny had to make herself reach out. Much to her astonishment and relief, the strong, thin legs of the unborn foal felt warm and alive in her hands.

The next contraction came. "Good," said Michael. "Pull firmly, and down toward the mare's hocks." The foal didn't move; Mokey rested.

Ginny braced herself. With the next contraction, she gave another pull and the foal slipped gently out onto the straw.

Ginny sat back on her heels and stared at the bundle of head and body and legs lying still in its membrane covering. "Quickly now," said Michael sharply. "Break the membrane at its head."

Ginny tugged gently at the membrane, which looked so fragile, and was astonished at how strong it was. She yanked at it with frantic fingers and it tore silently. Ginny pulled it away from the foal's tiny muzzle. Its head looked strange as it appeared out of its covering shroud; its eyes were shut and its thin ears were limp.

Michael handed Ginny the armload of folded towels which had been ready on the shelf in the tack room. Ginny rubbed the foal's wet head and wiped out its nostrils.

The foal didn't move. It lay in a motionless, soggy heap on the straw without showing the slightest flicker of life. "It's dead!" Ginny said in a thin, shaky voice.

"Rub its sides," said Michael as he pulled the membrane back. "Hard. Don't worry, it's not as fragile as it looks." Ginny snatched a fresh towel and began to rub the foal's narrow body vigorously.

"Breathe," she whispered fiercely. She pressed more weight on the thin little ribs, rubbing the wet flanks harder and harder with the rough towel.

"All right," said Michael. Ginny stopped and looked up at him blankly, then turned her head to see why he was smiling. The foal's funny little head was raised completely off the straw and it was blinking at her from blurry eyes as though waking up from a long, deep sleep.

"Well, hi," said Ginny, sitting back on her heels. The foal sneezed and its head collapsed back onto the straw.

"Fantastic," said Ginny. Kneeling beside the foal, she watched its flanks fluttering, more and more steadily, as its breathing grew stronger.

"Very nice," said Michael, his thin face split in a wide grin.

Ginny went on drying the foal, more gently, and gradually her mind stopped whirling and the rest of her surroundings came slowly back into focus. Mokey was lying perfectly still, just as she'd been when the foal was born. She was breathing gently with a strange, faraway look in her eyes, almost as though she were in a trance.

"Is she O.K.?" Ginny asked Michael anxiously.

Michael nodded. "Just let her alone. She's resting," he said.

The foal made a sudden effort, put out one thin foreleg, and rolled to an upright position. Ginny beamed at it proudly. Gradually, almost unbelievingly, she realized what she'd been far too busy to notice before: the foal was not spotted in uneven patches like its mother—it wasn't spotted at all. It was a solid, rich brown with a blazing white star on its forehead.

"Shouldn't I be doing something?" Ginny asked Michael. "What about the umbilical cord? Shouldn't it be cut?"

"Let it be," said Michael. "It will break when the mare gets up."

Mokey turned her head slowly, pricked her ears, and gave a soft, murmuring sound, deep in her throat. To Ginny's astonishment, the foal answered with a quavering whinny.

Mokey surged to her feet and turned to peer suspiciously at her newborn foal. Ginny retreated to the side of the stall so she wouldn't be in the way. Mokey snuffled and blew at the damp little creature lying in her straw. It was clear that she was puzzled and uncertain. She put back her ears and stamped her foot.

The foal's heavy head bobbed and weaved at the end of its short neck. Mokey reached out to nuzzle its shoulder and then gave it a gentle nudge with her muzzle. The foal tipped over onto its side and Mokey jumped back in fright.

"Dumb pony," Ginny said disgustedly. "Doesn't she recognize her own baby? Why is she behaving like this?"

"Just give her a chance," said Michael. "All this is new to her." He got Mokey's halter and handed it to Ginny. "Put this on her and hold her for a minute. Talk to her and pat her and let her know that everything is all right."

The foal gave another squeaky whinny and struggled halfway to its feet. Mokey jerked the halter out of Ginny's hands and flew to the far side of the stall. Michael brought a lead rope, Ginny recaptured her pony, and the foal collapsed in a tangled heap with a despairing little squeal.

Ginny looked worriedly at Michael, but he seemed totally unconcerned. Whistling softly under his breath, he brought the bottle of iodine from the shelf in the tack room, soaked a piece of cotton in it, and pressed it against the stump of the umbilical cord on the foal's stomach. "It's a colt," he said to Ginny over his shoulder.

Mokey snorted at the sharp smell of the iodine. The foal tried to stand up again. This time he almost made it before he fell. "He's going to hurt himself!" said Ginny.

Michael smiled and shook his head. Ginny held Mokey, stroking her shoulder gently with one hand, and they all watched in silence as the colt rested and then tried once more to stand up.

Chapter Twelve

Five minutes later the colt was standing perilously on all four legs, swaying from side to side. "Great," Ginny said proudly. The colt took a single tottering step and collapsed again. Mokey jumped and squealed and stamped her foot.

"Oh, cut it out, Mokey!" Ginny said. "What kind of a mother are you, anyway?"

Mokey subsided, looking sour. "She doesn't really understand yet," said Michael. "She's confused and a little bit frightened. This is her first foal; give her a chance to get used to the idea."

The colt scrambled to his feet and walked shakily toward his mother. Mokey's eyes widened and she backed away nervously.

"How long can he wait?" Ginny asked, struggling to hold Mokey still. "Isn't he hungry? Is Mokey going to hurt him if he tries to nurse?"

"She might just now, if we weren't here," said Michael. "But we're not going to let that happen. That's enough foolishness, Mokey. Like it or not, this little fellow is your responsibility."

He scooped the staggering little foal up in his arms. "Hold her with one hand and pick her foreleg up with the other," Michael said to Ginny. After a brief struggle, Ginny managed to do as she had been told. Michael carried the colt over to Mokey's side and steadied him gently while he groped blindly for his milk.

Mokey squealed and switched her tail uneasily as the colt started to nurse. "Is she trying to kick?" asked Ginny.

"She might if she could, but she can't while you're holding her foreleg up," said Michael.

The colt nursed clumsily at first. Michael held him patiently while the colt struggled to control all four of his legs and his first attempts at nursing at the same time. It was difficult and complicated, and more than once he started to tip over and fall, but Michael's quiet hands were there to steady him and Ginny held Mokey still. Gradually the foal grew stronger and more sure of himself; Mokey seemed less tense and frightened. At Michael's nod, Ginny let Mokey's foreleg down gently and the pony turned her head and softly nuzzled the flanks of her foal.

The colt stopped nursing. His legs buckled and he swung his head away from his mother. There were white drops of milk all over his small muzzle. His large, dark eyes were half closed and his white-starred head swayed weakly from side to side.

"What's the matter with him?" asked Ginny in a panic.

Michael smiled. "He's sleepy," he said. He eased the foal down onto the straw.

Mokey, stiff-legged, made a circle around the stall, and then put her head down to sniff the foal from head to tail. Almost shyly she put out her tongue and licked his shoulder.

"She's getting braver," Ginny whispered. Mokey blew softly through flared nostrils. The foal lifted his head, nickered drowsily, and then fell asleep. Mokey nudged him with her muzzle and jumped back; the foal didn't move.

With an enormous sigh, Mokey stood quietly

over her foal. Her head dropped so that her muzzle was almost touching his shoulder and her eyes closed.

The foal was still damp and he was starting to shiver. Ginny tiptoed into the tack room and turned on the heat lamps. They bathed the sleeping foal in a pool of warm light.

"Take Mokey's halter off," Michael told Ginny in a low voice. "It's risky leaving a halter on a mare with a foal; there's always the chance of his getting a foreleg caught in it."

Shivering at the very thought, Ginny moved quietly into the stall, slipped Mokey's halter off, and looked down with weary pride at the foal in the straw.

"Let them rest," said Michael. Ginny left the stall and gently pulled the door almost shut behind her, leaving it open just enough for them to watch.

Twenty minutes later the foal woke up, stretched luxuriously, and scrambled strongly to his feet. Ginny started into the stall with Mokey's halter, but Michael gestured for her to wait.

The colt teetered around his mother. Mokey stood still, watching him anxiously, but she didn't move as the colt butted his small head in annoyance against her flank as he searched for his milk. Mokey squealed softly but didn't kick, and in a moment the foal was nursing busily with his short, curly tail whisking from side to side.

As the minutes passed, Mokey lost her worried look. She turned her head and nuzzled the nursing foal's hindquarters with a tender, loving gesture.

Ginny hadn't realized she'd been holding her

breath. She let it out with a long sigh of relief. "I guess she knows it's hers, now," she said.

Michael was watching with warm approval. "No doubt about it, she's accepted him as her own. And that's a nice colt, Miss Ginny. He's going to be well worth raising. Too bad we don't know the breeding of the sire. There's real quality there."

Ginny squinted her eyes thoughtfully, nodded, and then laughed. "I suppose you must be right," she said, "but I think he's beautiful just because he's here."

Mrs. Anderson came home and was very disappointed to hear she'd missed the birth. Dr. Nichols came soon after, spinning into the driveway looking harried and anxious, but Ginny told him quickly that everything was all right. They all went quietly down to the stable together.

Mokey didn't like having them there. She swung herself neatly between the open doorway and her foal, hiding him from sight.

"*Now* what's the matter with her?" Ginny said crossly. "First she won't let him near her, and now she won't let us see him!"

Michael and Dr. Nichols agreed that none of this was in the least unusual, especially in a mare with her first foal. Ginny put a halter on Mokey and held her tightly while the doctor examined the foal and gave him a tetanus and antibiotic shot while Michael held him, then watched as the little colt capered across the stall, back to his frantic mother.

"She'll settle down in a few days," the doctor assured Ginny. "You can let them outside in the paddock for a few minutes tomorrow, if the weather's warm."

When everyone had left a few minutes later, Ginny gave the stall a thorough cleaning, filled Mokey's bucket with fresh water, emptied the uneaten grain from her feed tub, and went to make the pony a fresh hot mash as Dr. Nichols had told her to do.

She glanced at her watch as she made her way up to the house. It was barely noon. It seemed impossible, after all those dreary, endless weeks of waiting, all those sleepless nights and tiresome days, that everything had happened and was over in such an incredibly short time.

She sat down for a minute on the kitchen steps,

going over in her mind all the instructions Dr. Nichols had given her. The white snowdrops were gone from the protected corner beside the steps and yellow and purple crocuses bloomed in their place. In the hazy light of the spring sun, the buds of the blossoms on the apple tree next to the kitchen window were starting to swell and turn pink. Ginny chewed thoughtfully on the end of one braid. Spring was everywhere now; it had been almost a year since Mokey had come.

Ginny closed her eyes dreamily. What should she name the new foal? She pictured the sturdy little red-bay colt with his pretty head and blazing white star. Maybe she should call him Starlight—

A bird flew down and hopped busily across the lawn under the apple tree. Ginny watched it for a moment. She wanted a spring name for Mokey's new foal—

Ginny stood up. The bird flew away with its red breast flashing over the soft green of the new spring grass.

"I'm going to call him Robin," Ginny said out loud. In a daze of happy weariness, she went into the house to cut up some carrots for Mokey's mash.